BE A MAKER!

Maker Projects for Kids Who Love

SPORTS

SARAH LEVETE

 Crabtree Publishing Company
www.crabtreebooks.com

Crabtree Publishing Company

www.crabtreebooks.com

Author: Sarah Levete

Series research and development: Reagan Miller

Editors: Sarah Eason, and Philip Gebhardt

Proofreader: Wendy Scavuzzo

Editorial director: Kathy Middleton

Design: Paul Myerscough

Layout: Keith Williams

Cover design: Paul Myerscough

Photo research: Rachel Blount

Production coordinator and prepress technician:
Tammy McGarr

Print coordinator: Margaret Amy Salter

Consultant: Jennifer Turliuk, CEO MakerKids

Production coordinated by Calcium Creative

Photo Credits:

t=Top, bl=Bottom Left, br=Bottom Right

Getty Images: Katherine Frey/The Washington Post via Getty Images:
p. 15; Cristina Mittermeier/National Geographic: p. 19; Shutterstock:
Martynova Anna: p. 24; Aspen Photo: p. 7; Maxim Blinkov: pp. 1,
23; CP DC Press: p. 14; ESB Essentials: p. 9; Melinda Fawver: p. 16;
HodagMedia: p. 6; Susan Leggett: p. 4; Tom Lester: p. 8; Muzsy: p. 26;
NadyaEugene: p. 18; Pio3: p. 22; A. Ricardo: p. 10; Wavebreakmedia: p. 5;
Leonard Zhukovsky: p. 25; Tudor Photography: pp. 12–13, 20–21, 28–29;
Wikimedia Commons: MartinPutz: p. 17; Michael Pick from Brooklyn,
United States: p. 11; United Nations: p. 27

Cover: Tudor Photography.

Library and Archives Canada Cataloguing in Publication

Levete, Sarah, author
    Maker projects for kids who love sports / Sarah Levete.

(Be a maker!)
Includes index.
Issued in print and electronic formats.
ISBN 978-0-7787-2877-1 (hardcover).--
ISBN 978-0-7787-2891-7 (softcover).--
ISBN 978-1-4271-1909-4 (HTML)

    1. Sports--Juvenile literature. I. Title. II. Series: Be a
maker!

GV705.4.L48 2017   j796   C2016-907372-6
                                   C2016-907373-4

Library of Congress Cataloging-in-Publication Data

Names: Levete, Sarah, author.
Title: Maker Projects for Kids Who Love Sports / Sarah Levete.
Description: New York : Crabtree Publishing Company, 2017. |
   Series: Be a Maker! | Includes index. |
Identifiers: LCCN 2016050612 (print) | LCCN 2016058114 (ebook)
   ISBN 9780778728771 (reinforced library binding) |
   ISBN 9780778728917 (pbk.) |
   ISBN 9781427119094 (Electronic HTML)
Subjects: LCSH: Sports--Juvenile literature. | Makerspaces--
   Juvenile literature.
Classification: LCC GV705.4 L47 2017 (print) |
   LCC GV705.4 (ebook) | DDC 796--dc23
LC record available at https://lccn.loc.gov/2016050612

Crabtree Publishing Company

www.crabtreebooks.com   1-800-387-7650

Printed in Canada/022017/CH20161214

Published in Canada
Crabtree Publishing
616 Welland Ave.
St. Catharines, Ontario
L2M 5V6

Published in the United States
Crabtree Publishing
PMB 59051
350 Fifth Avenue, 59th Floor
New York, New York 10118

Published in the United Kingdom
Crabtree Publishing
Maritime House
Basin Road North, Hove
BN41 1WR

Published in Australia
Crabtree Publishing
3 Charles Street
Coburg North
VIC, 3058

CONTENTS

GET IN THE GAME!

Sports are good for fun, fitness, and friends! Taking part in sports improves physical and mental strength, and **resilience**. Some people play team sports to win. But more often than not, taking part is what counts. Sports present individual challenges, whether it is working as a team or pushing your body to new limits.

THE MAKER MOVEMENT

The maker movement is all about trying new things and creating new possibilities. Use your imagination, practical skills, and sense of adventure to apply your maker spirit to your favorite sports. **Collaborate** with your friends and visit a local **makerspace** to come up with and share new ideas and approaches to sports. Play it, and own it!

Join in any sport to stretch your body and to challenge the limits of what you believe you can do.

BEING A MAKER

- Makers are willing to take risks and understand that failure is an important part of the process.
- Makers are persistent and do not give up easily.
- Makers are **resourceful**. They look for materials and **inspiration** in unlikely places.
- Makers take on responsibility. They enjoy working on projects that can help others.
- Makers support each other and feel positive. They believe that small things can make an important difference in the world.

All of these qualities are important to remember while participating in any sport.

When you take up a sport, it can take time to master new techniques. Learning new skills with friends is a great way to get started!

SAFETY FIRST

Sports involve physical activity that is good for your health. It is a good idea to get a health check from your doctor before starting a sport, especially if you have any injuries or medical concerns. Some sports require specific skills before you can start, such as learning how to swim before hitting the pool on your own. If you are **adapting** a sport, ask a responsible adult to make sure it is safe.

Be a Maker!

You do not even need equipment other than your body and enthusiasm for sports! Run, jog, twist, shuffle, jump, or turn—how many ways can you use your body for sports?

HISTORY OF SPORTS

Wrestling, boxing, hunting, archery, and running are some of the earliest recorded sports. Many of these sports were linked to survival skills—humans tracked and hunted animals to provide food for their families. In ancient Greece, men and boys trained in **gymnasiums** for military duty.

A FUNNY KIND OF BALL

Soccer, one of today's most popular sports, had its beginnings in China during the second century B.C.E. According to records, men training for the army played a game in which a "ball" was kicked around with the aim of getting it into a goal. In those days, the ball was made from an **inflated** pig bladder! During the 1300s in England, soccer became such a popular street game that the king banned it! He thought people were spending too much time playing soccer and not enough on practicing archery—a skill that was more useful for winning wars.

Bicycle races have been popular for hundreds of years. In this picture from the 1800s, riders race on towering bikes with large front wheels. This type of bicycle was called a penny farthing.

AN ANCIENT HISTORY

Lacrosse is a fast-paced team sport. Players use long sticks with mesh pockets to catch, carry, and throw a ball. Hundreds of years ago in North America, the Iroquois began playing the game as a way to physically prepare men and boys for war. Sometimes more than 1,000 people took part in games that lasted for days and spread out over many miles. Local settlers began to play the game, too, and it soon became popular across Canada and the United States.

Lacrosse players run and sprint, throw and catch. It is a great team sport that keeps players fit and focused.

INFORMAL OR ORGANIZED?

Sports can be played **recreationally**, **competitively**, informally, or formally in organized **leagues** or groups. Some athletes are paid to train and take part in their chosen sport. They are known as **professionals**. Recreational athletes play for fun. As a sport develops and becomes more popular, participants often set up organizing bodies that set out the rules and regulations for the sport. These organizations also set standards for training and competition.

Be a Maker!

Many early sports made use of everyday materials that were readily available. Take a look around your house or school for items that could inspire a new game. What kind of sport could you play with a broom or a pair of rolled-up socks? Ask an adult for permission before you try out any new sports equipment.

FIT AND FUN

According to the United Nations Inter-Agency Task Force on Sport for Development and Peace, sports are, "all forms of physical activity that contribute to physical fitness, mental well-being, and social interaction, such as play, recreation, organized or competitive sport, and **indigenous** sports and games." One person may enjoy a relaxing game of golf, while another person loves a strenuous workout in the gym—they are both sports, yet they are very different!

IMPORTANCE OF SPORTS

Taking part in a sport has benefits for the brain and body, including:

- Improving your physical fitness by helping you develop strong muscles and bones.
- Improving **cardiovascular** health, so you will have a stronger, healthier heart.
- Improving social skills, such as teamwork and taking responsibility.
- Developing perseverance. Any sport will throw challenges at you—it is about meeting them head-on.

Rock climbing presents the climber with physical and mental challenges.

SOMETHING FOR EVERYONE

There is one thing common to all sports—the people who take part! Without participants or players, there is no sport. Some sports, such as basketball, need a team. Others, such as swimming or track and field, are individual sports, but can also be enjoyed by a group or competitive team. It is great to watch a sport, be a fan, and cheer on your team, but it is even better to get out there and get involved.

To take your pulse, place two fingers under your chin as shown. Feel for a steady beat. Count the beats for 15 seconds, then multiply the number by 4.

Be a Maker!

Time to get your heart pumping! A circuit is a series of activities that involves rotating through different kinds of exercises, usually for a set period of time. With a group of friends and adult supervision, head out to the playground or to the school gym. Have each person choose a station and come up with one activity for it. Include a mix of activities that focus on different motions, such as jumping and squatting. Do a few jumping jacks to warm up, then have everyone rotate through the circuit, spending one minute at each station. After one complete rotation, try adding new challenges to the activities, such as working in pairs. Make sure to have water on hand to stay hydrated. Stretch well after the workout.

GET EQUIPPED!

Most sports need some kind of equipment. When playing for fun, you can use any equipment that is handy, but in more organized leagues, equipment often plays a key part in success. From ensuring players' safety to enhancing an athlete's performance, makers are always looking for innovative ways to improve a sport.

SCIENCE AND SPORTS

Scientists are always looking for new ways to improve equipment for performance and comfort. German champion cyclist Denise Schindler wears a **prosthetic** leg made on a 3-D printer. It was designed to be lightweight and **aerodynamic**. The winning British cycling team in the 2016 **Olympic Games** in Rio de Janeiro rode on bicycles that were designed for speed and efficiency. Even the paint of the bikes was specially developed with a super-smooth coating to make it as aerodynamic as possible. The science behind the paint remains a secret, but **Formula 1** teams want to use it on their cars, too!

A cyclist wears a long, tapered helmet and tight-fitting clothes to be as aerodynamic as possible.

10

GET CREATIVE

Professional basketball players use balls that have been designed, engineered, and manufactured using special materials to **optimize** speed and bounce. There are even "smart" balls with sensors that can transmit data, such as how many baskets a player sinks, to devices 90 feet (27 m) away. Many professional tennis players have their rackets **custom-made**. But you do not need a fancy ball or racket to enjoy a sport. Can you make your own racket with some string or stretchy old clothes? Make a frame, then experiment with different materials for the strings.

Makers and Shakers

Jacques Plante

French-Canadian Jacques Plante (1929–1986) was a fearless hockey goalie who played for the Montreal Canadiens. However, in 1959, at a game at Madison Square Garden, Plante was hit in the face by a puck. His nose was broken and he needed stitches. Although his coach thought that the goalie's injuries showed guts and bravery, Plante was determined not to get hurt again. He said he would only play if he could wear a protective **fiberglass** mask that he used in practice. At first, he was mocked for the protective gear, but today all NHL goalies wear masks.

Jacques Plante's original mask is on display at the Hockey Hall of Fame in Toronto, Canada.

Plante, Jacques #1

MAKE IT!
CRISSCROSS BOOMERANG

A boomerang is a curved piece of sports equipment. It was traditionally used as a hunting tool by the indigenous peoples of Australia. When it is thrown, it travels through the air in a curve, then returns to the thrower. Make your own three-armed boomerang using different materials to see which material helps your boomerang fly the best!

YOU WILL NEED
- Heavy card stock, and other kinds of paper, such as cardboard and watercolor paper
- Scissors
- Tape
- Glue
- Colored pencils or pens
- Glitter glue
- 360 degree protractor. (This is not essential, but is helpful for measuring the angle of the boomerang arms.)
- Pencil

- Decide on the shape of your boomerang's arm. Draw it on the card stock.
- Cut out the arm.
- Now use the arm to trace two more arms for each boomerang you want to make.
- Try to make sure each arm is exactly the same shape.
- Cut out the arms.

1

2

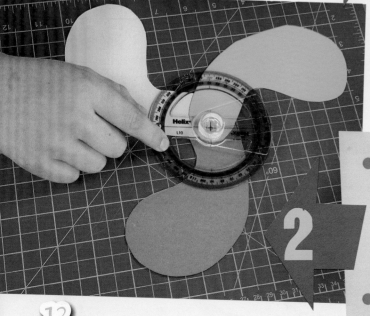

- Use your 360 degree protractor to measure the distance between the arms on your boomerang. You need to have the arms at 120 degree angles. This will help you make an effective boomerang that will return when you throw it.
- Once you are happy with the angles and distance, tape the arms together.

3

- Once the arms are taped together, decorate the boomerang.
- You can use any type of decoration you like. Why not color your boomerang with pens or pencils, or add glitter glue?

- Find a safe area to test out your boomerang. How well does it fly?
- Next, try making more boomerangs from different types of paper. Try heavy cardboard, then try a lighter paper, such as watercolor paper. What is the difference between the types of boomerangs when you test them out? Which flies the best?

4

CONCLUSION

Once you have thrown your boomerang several times, take a look at it. How well has it survived its flight? Did the boomerang return to you as planned, or did it land too quickly? To improve its performance, what changes can you make to the shape or measurements of the boomerang, or the way you throw it?

Make It Even Better!

What different materials or shapes can you use to create a sturdier boomerang? How could you use your boomerang to play a team sport? By what standard will you measure the success of each boomerang?

SPORTS EQUALS

In the past, many organized sports were only open to boys and men. There were fewer opportunities for girls to take part in sports. Some sports, such as wrestling, were considered boys' sports. Others, such as gymnastics, were considered more suitable for girls. Today great strides are being made toward leveling the playing field, regardless of gender.

GIRL POWER!

Maria Toorpakai Wazir loved sports from a young age. However, girls in Pakistan were not allowed to play sports. For a long time, Maria pretended to be a boy so she could take part in sports. However, with determination and her family's support, Maria is now a top-ranked professional squash player. At age 13, American Mo'ne Davis made sports history as the first girl to pitch a **shutout** at the Little League World Series. She throws hard, with her fastball flying from the mound at more than 70 miles per hour (115 km/h).

From wrestling to weightlifting, girls are now able to take part in any sport.

In true maker style, Keeling Pilaro has shown resilience to continue playing the sport he loves, despite criticism from others.

Makers and Shakers

Keeling Pilaro

Field hockey is a popular sport all over the world. The United States has a men's national team and a women's national team. But in many parts of the country, at lower levels of play, field hockey is considered to be a girls' sport. Keeling Pilaro (born 1998) is one player working to change that **perception**. He started playing field hockey in Ireland. When his family returned to the United States, 12-year-old Pilaro joined the team at his new school. He was the only boy on the **roster**, and his right to play was challenged many times. Pilaro's teammates and coach supported him. By his second season, the team uniform was changed to shorts instead of the traditional skirt. A ruling by the local athletic governing body eventually benched Pilaro from official games, but he has not let that stop him. He now attends a boarding school, continues to train with the girls' team, and helps coach. He dreams of one day playing on the men's national team and at the Olympics.

WINNING WAYS

What does winning mean? Is it the person who crosses the finish line first, or the person who has pushed himself or herself to their limit? Winning means different things to different people. In some activities, such as working out in the gym, there is no competitive element unless you are challenging yourself.

FOLLOW THE RULES

Rules and regulations in a sport keep it fair and safe for all participants. Everyone has the same chance in a sport if there are clear guidelines and a level, or fair playing field. When you play a game of baseball, you and your friends probably agree on rules. Informal or recreational sports, such as kicking a ball with your friends in the park or a game of street hockey, often have some generally accepted rules.

In a race, runners wear chips that record their individual times. This provides everyone with a level playing field, no matter what order they cross the finish line.

SPORTING SPIRIT

There are lots of ways to show you are a winner, and it does not always mean coming first. In a grueling **triathlon** race in Mexico, competitor Jonny Brownlee was in first place. But in the home stretch, he began to lose pace as he had overexerted himself in the earlier stages of the race. His brother Alistair was also competing. Instead of carrying on, Alistair stopped to help his stumbling brother cross the finish line. At the 2016 Olympic Games in Rio, American athlete Abbey D'Agostino and New Zealand's Nikki Hamblin tumbled over each other. Instead of continuing the race, D'Agostino stopped to help her competitor complete the course, saying, in true maker style: "Get up, we have to finish this." What could be more winning than the spirit of these competitors?

In 2016, the Brownlee brothers were both included in the top-ten list of the world's best male triathletes.

Be a Maker!

Get together with a group of friends. Come up with some ideas for a new sport, or a variation of an existing sport. Think about whether this sport is for individuals, to be played as a team, purely for fun, or if it is to be competitive. On what terrain does it take place—land, air, or water? How can you ensure that everyone taking part has an equal turn at the sport? How can you make sure that it is safe and fair? Think about other sports and their rules. Can you learn from your experience by following, or even challenging, existing rules?

MAKE DO

You do not need to speak the same language or have the same background to enjoy and share the fun of a sport. Anyone can join a game of catch. Some sports, such as car racing and horseback riding, are traditionally associated with wealth. Access to these sports is more limited. However, there are many sports open to everyone, and there are lots of ways to get around any obstacles that you may face.

PLAYING FIELD

There are sports that take place on or in water, sports that take place in the air, and sports that take place on land. Obviously, you need ice for ice hockey—but you can play street hockey pretty much anywhere! If you cannot get to a gym, think how you can turn your local park into an outdoor gym! If you do not have a court, mark out some lines with chalk or use cones to mark a field of play. Remember, always check that the area is suitable for the activity so that you and your friends stay safe.

With chalk, mark out some squares and play a game of hopscotch with friends!

MEETING CHALLENGES

Being a maker builds on your ability to respond to unexpected situations, to **improvise**, think on your feet, develop strategies, and have fun with items at hand. Make such challenges work to your advantage. Use your imagination to enjoy sports wherever you are, and with whatever equipment you have on hand. In some parts of the world, where people have limited access to equipment and limited money, they make their own balls from plastic bags! They scrunch together lots of plastic bags and bind them tightly with string. They are great to hit, throw, catch, and kick. (Just make sure to keep the bags you use away from small children, and wrap the string around your ball tightly and securely.) Try it and see what sports you can play with your new ball!

Resourceful young boys in India play a game of soccer with a homemade ball. What other materials could be used to make a soccer ball?

Makers and Shakers

Walter Frederick Morrison

At age 17, while at a picnic, Walter Frederick Morrison (1920–2010) started tossing the lid of a popcorn tin back and forth with his girlfriend. The pair soon discovered that a pie tin was better suited to the activity. The popularity of tossing the tin led Morrison to invent the Pluto Platter—a flat, plastic disc, named after the popularity of flying saucers at the time. Eventually the disc was renamed to what it is known as today—the Frisbee!

19

MAKE IT!
RULE BOOK

Make your own Frisbee shootout game! Use these suggestions to inspire you and get you started on making a rule book for a sport that you create. Working with a group of friends will help you problem solve as you play.

Follow some basic rules. Here are some to get you started:
- One goalkeeper, and one shooter.
- The shooter stands around the penalty marker on the soccer field. If there is no penalty marker, then choose a spot where both players agree it is fair for the shooter to throw from.
- The shooter has five shots to try to get the Frisbee in the net.
- The goalkeeper has five chances to block the Frisbee shots.
- The shooter can move left and right, but cannot pass the marker.
- *Remember, these are suggestions only—you can come up with your own basic rules!* Try out the rules and note them in your rule book. Change them as you like until you have rules you are happy with.

Now for the next rules! How are you going to score? You could try this idea, or come up with your own method:
- When the Frisbee goes into the net, the shooter gets a point. The shooter must note how many shots out of five he or she gets in the net.
- If the Frisbee shot goes over the net, that counts as a miss.
- Try out your scoring rules, then note them in your rule book.

How will you decide the winner? Here are some ideas to get you started:

- Once the shooter has shot five times, the goalkeeper and the shooter switch positions.
- The first goalkeeper is now the shooter, and the first shooter is now in net. Play again with each player in their new position so everyone has an equal opportunity to win.
- If the new shooter gets more shots in, he or she is the winner. If the new shooter gets fewer in, the first shooter is the victor!
- Try out your scoring system, recording in your notebook what works well and what does not work.

3

4

- Once you are happy as a team that your game works, use your notes to write up your rule book.
- How does your rule book look?

Make It Even Better!

Once you have a rule book for your sport, think about ways that you could improve it. How could you make the sport more challenging? Could you use different equipment to play, such as a hockey net?

CONCLUSION

Discuss with your team if you think the rule book has provided the guidance that is needed for this activity, or if there are ways you and your team need to adapt it. Have someone else read the rule book. How well is the sport explained? Ask for feedback to make sure the rules clearly explain the activity.

GOING TO EXTREMES

Just when you think a sport has reached an extreme, another wild and wacky sport is invented that offers a whole new level of adventure! Extreme sports challenge the physical and mental strength of an athlete. These sports are risky, and should not be attempted without supervision by a responsible adult. Some sports that began as "extreme sports" have become fixtures in sporting events. You can ride a bike to school or to see your friends. On the other hand, you can take cycling to new extremes by riding a bike up and down muddy trails, across streams, and over steep drops. Whichever type of cycling you want to go for, it is a must to wear a helmet!

People who participate in parkour are called traceurs (boys) or traceuses (girls).

RUNNING FREE

Parkour, also known as free running, was created in France in the 1980s. Parkour is about moving across and over any ground using only your body. This can involve jumping, running, swinging, and climbing. Parkour is generally done in urban areas—no equipment is needed. The sport pairs creativity with a fun workout. People who participate in parkour train with experienced adults, since this sport can be dangerous.

FLYING HIGH

Flying a kite is a relaxing sport—or is it? In Thailand, kite flying is a serious sport with kite fights taking to the skies during competitions. Teams try to bring down their opponent's kite. In India, players coat the kite string with ground glass, then try to cut the string of their opponent's kite as it soars through the air. Kites are now used in water sports, too. Kitesurfing combines kite, board, and waves. Catch some wind, and the kite will carry you over the waves.

Boards provide the opportunity to ride the waves, skate on the sidewalk, or glide on the snow. Can you think of other ways to use boards in sports?

Makers and Shakers

Sherman Poppen

Today, snowboarding is popular with young and old. On Christmas Day in 1964, inspiration struck when a young surfer named Sherman Poppen (born 1930) decided to build a surfboard for the snow! With true maker spirit, Poppen went to his garage and bolted his children's skis together. His daughter took to the snow and "snurfed." When Poppen realized how popular it was, he started making more boards, and added a rope to help the rider balance. Poppen wisely **patented** the idea. Later inventions based on the snurfboard led to today's snowboard.

SPORTS FOR ALL

Anyone can take part in sports. Adaptive sports are designed for people with physical or intellectual disabilities. They are often **modifications** of existing sports.

ATHLETIC EXCELLENCE

For athletes who excel in their chosen sport, events such as the Olympics are the place to put all their hard work and training to the test. The **Paralympics** are the second-largest sports competition in the world, featuring more than 4,350 athletes from 176 nations. Competitors are athletes with various disabilities. Sports are adapted as needed. The games include a range of sports from wheelchair tennis to tae kwan do, a **martial art**. Visually impaired athletes run with a guide. In the Rio Paralympics, blind athlete Abdellatif Baka of Algeria ran the 1500-meter race. Not only did he set a new Paralympic world record, he also ran the fastest 1500 meters of any athlete in Rio—able-bodied or disabled.

Whatever the sport, it can be adapted to suit the needs of the individual.

LEVELING THE FIELD

The Inclusion Club, an organization that spreads awareness about inclusivity in sports, lists six ways sports or equipment can be adapted for disabled athletes, including:

- Size: Use a smaller or larger ball, or lower a net.
- Speed: A slower ball can be more accessible. Adding weight can slow it down.
- Surface: Add lights or texture to the surface of the playing area or equipment to help players orient themselves or improve grip.
- Support: Use a support, such as a string attached to a ball, to make it more accessible.
- Sound: Add sound to equipment to support visually impaired players. This can be done easily by taping a bell to a ball or net.
- Switch: Create a switch to release a ball or to swing a bat or racket.

In Paralympic tennis, rules are modified. The ball can bounce twice on an opponent's side of the court, rather than just once.

Be a Maker!

Get together with some friends. Think about how you might make a sport more user-friendly. Who are you adapting it for—older people, younger children, or people with a disability? Is the equipment the challenge, or do the rules need to be changed? The solution may lie in a simple adjustment, such as lowering a net, or it may require a complete rethink. When you have come up with an idea, test it out. Brainstorm ways to adapt a sport so that teams are made up of both able-bodied and disabled players.

CHANGING LIVES

Nelson Mandela (1918–2013) once said: "Sport has the power to change the world. It has the power to inspire. It has the power to unite people in a way that little else does. It speaks to youth in a language they understand." As the leader of South Africa from 1994 to 1999, Mandela believed that sports could help unite the country. South Africa had previously been divided by race under a system called **apartheid**. Under the new government, black players and white players can play rugby on the same team. One of many ways the country attempted to unite after decades of division was through sports.

TEAM SPIRIT

Team sports not only help to keep you fit, they also improve other skills. You need to communicate well in a team sport to be aware of your teammate's next move. You need to share ideas—only a team that discusses **tactics** and performance will work effectively when playing. Sports can help you make friends, and take on new challenges. Discover the joys of playing, and celebrate others when they win.

Sports are about sharing success, encouraging others, learning from defeat, and respecting fellow players.

FINDING A WAY

Sports are full of inspiring stories. Eighteen-year-old swimmer Yusra Mardini and her sister fled their home country, war-torn Syria. Their journey from their native country to Europe was traumatic. As the boat she and other **refugees** were on started to sink, Mardini and her sister jumped into the water. For more than two hours, the sisters and two other refugees swam, pushing the boat and its occupants safely to shore. Just four years later, Mardini swam on Team Refugee at the 2016 Olympic Games.

Yusra Mardini found ways to keep swimming, despite the most challenging circumstances.

Be a Maker!

In some communities, sporting events draw people together, while also bringing awareness to a cause. Relay for Life is a walk that raises funds for cancer research. The Warrior Dash is an obstacle-course race that has donated more than $13 million to St. Jude's Children's Research Hospital. Think about ways you can combine your love of sports with helping others. Brainstorm ideas with your friends or classmates. What local cause can you support? How can you help spread the word? Work together to plan an event at your school or in your local community.

MAKE IT!
OBSTACLE-COURSE RELAY RACE

YOU WILL NEED
- Two hula hoops
- Two skipping ropes
- Six pylons
- Six beanbags
- Two buckets to toss the beanbags in
- Participants—at least four people, two on each team
- Timer—you can use a stopwatch or your cell phone

Outdoors or indoors, you can make a great obstacle course for individuals or teams. The materials listed and instructions on these pages are for inspiration— make up your own obstacle course with whatever materials you have on hand.

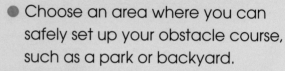

1

- Choose an area where you can safely set up your obstacle course, such as a park or backyard.
- You will need two lanes—one for each team.
- Set up each lane with your obstacles. Put the obstacles at equal intervals in each lane, and set up the same obstacle at the same stage of each lane. You can have anywhere from three to five, six, or seven obstacles in each lane! Use your imagination!

Determine what each participant has to do at each station. For example:
- Zigzag through the pylons.
- Skip ten times.
- Hula hoop ten times.
- Toss the three beanbags into the bucket.
- Jog back to the start and tag the next person.

2

3

- Decide who is going to be on each team. Make sure everyone knows what to do at each obstacle.
- Decide who will run first, second, third, or last, depending on how many racers you have on each team.

- Once all team members are in position at the starting point, the race can begin.
- Start the race, and time the run. When the first person finishes the course, they will run back to the starting point and tag the hand of their teammate.
- Note the time the last runner in each team returns to the starting point. Which team won?

4

Make It Even Better!

Sports are all about challenges. What new obstacles could you add to the course that require different skills? Does the course work well for a relay team, or would it be better as an individual race? Would running the course in pairs be challenging? Could changing the order of the obstacles make it easier for younger children to participate? How could you adapt the course for a person who is visually impaired?

CONCLUSION

Once you and your teammates have caught your breath, ask each other what you thought of the course. Do parts of the course need revising or adapting to make it safer or more challenging? How can you address these concerns?

GLOSSARY

adapting Changing to function better

aerodynamic Having a shape that reduces resistance as it moves through the air

apartheid A South African government policy that separated people based on race; it was abolished in 1994

cardiovascular Having to do with the heart and blood vessels

collaborate Work together

competitively Competing against someone else

custom-made Made to meet specific needs

fiberglass A strong, lightweight material made from plastic and thin threads of glass

Formula 1 International auto racing in single-seat cars

gymnasiums Spaces used for fitness and sports

improvise To make or invent something using whatever is available

indigenous Growing, living, or occurring naturally in a particular place

inflated Filled and made larger with air or gas

inspiration Something that gives you ideas for something you want to make or do

leagues Groups of sports teams that regularly play against each other

makerspace A place where makers meet to share ideas, innovate, and invent

martial art A sport that was originally used as a form of self-defense, usually associated with China and Japan

modifications Changes made to something

Olympic Games A global sporting competition, held every four years, that celebrates sporting excellence

optimize To make something as good as possible

Paralympics A global sporting competition, held every four years, to celebrate sporting excellence for athletes with disabilities

patented Obtained legal ownership of an idea or invention

perception How something is understood

professional Someone who is paid to take part in a sport or activity

prosthetic An artificial device that replaces a missing body part

recreationally Done for enjoyment

refugees People who flee their country due to violence, war, or a natural disaster

resilience The ability to keep trying, despite challenges

resourceful Able to deal with new or difficult situations, and find solutions to problems

roster A list of people on a team

shutout A game in which one side does not score

tactics Plans for how to achieve something

triathlon A long-distance race with three events, such as swimming, cycling, and running

LEARNING MORE

BOOKS

Herzog, Brian. *Powerful Stories of Perseverance in Sports.* Free Spirit Publishing, 2014.

Raatma, Lucia. *The Curious, Captivating, Unusual History of Sports.* Capstone Press, 2012.

Swanson, Jennifer. *Super Gear: Nanotechnology and Sports Team Up.* Charlesbridge, 2016.

Wood, Alix. *Wacky Team Sports.* Gareth Stevens, 2014.

WEBSITES

Be inspired by other maker's unique sports:
https://diy.org/skills/athlete/challenges/1144/invent-an-athletic-game

Before trying a new sport, read about different kinds of equipment and safety pointers:
kidshealth.org/en/teens/sport-safety.html#

Visit the Inclusion Club website to learn about the ways creative makers are adapting sports for athletes of all abilities:
theinclusionclub.com/project/e52-adapt-it-sport-equipment-storeroom

Learn more about Paralympic sports:
www.timeforkids.com/news/paralympic-games/38121

INDEX

ABOUT THE AUTHOR

Sarah Levete has written dozens of books for children. She is an avid runner and swimmer who likes nothing more than playing a game of catch with her family.